JINGLES

AND THE
DARK NIGHT

For Elliot and Molly
Indiah, Madi and Phoebe

For Mrs Jingles who wandered into our lives
and made this possible.
M.F.

JINGLES

AND THE DARK NIGHT

Story by MARK FARMER

Illustrated by GAIL HANKS

Jingles woke up to the growling sound in the sky.

The box she was in was wet and starting to rip.

None of her brothers or sisters were with her!

THE WIND WAS HOWLING

and the lightning FLASHED,

THE RAIN POURED DOWN

and the THUNDER CRASHED!

Jingles didn't know what to do...

She climbed out of the box onto the cold, wet ground.

Lights were shining in the distance

and maybe that could be a warm place.

Suddenly something went past and Jingles

was soaked by lots of water.

She saw the red lights disappear into the distance.

THE WIND WAS HOWLING, and the lightning FLASHED, THE RAIN POURED DOWN and the THUNDER CRASHED!

Jingles didn't know what to do...

A strange noise came from the trees.

Jingles looked towards it and saw

two big bright eyes,

like the lights that had shone before.

The eyes swooped down towards her

and screeched over her head.

the WIND was HOWLING and the LIGHTNING FLASHED, the RAIN POURED DOWN and the THUNDER CRASHED!

Jingles didn't know what to do...

She ran as fast as she could into some bushes.

The rain didn't get her as much here.

She could still see some lights ahead.

They looked warm and safe.

Other little lights were shining in different colours

and she could hear lots of sounds.

THE WIND was HOWLING and the LIGHTNING FLASHED, THE RAIN POURED DOWN and the THUNDER CRASHED!

Jingles didn't know what to do...

The noises grew louder as she got closer to the lights.

People were dancing inside the warm building

and were laughing with each other.

Jingles could smell food inside.

She went closer to the door and was knocked back

by lots of feet and shouting people.

THE WIND WAS HOWLING
and the lightning FLASHED,
THE RAIN POURED DOWN
and the THUNDER CRASHED!

Jingles didn't know what to do...

She ran again

just missing the fast light.

Hiding in a doorway

Jingles felt sad.

Jingles felt lonely.

Jingles felt cold.

THE WIND WAS
HOWLING
and the lightning
FLASHED,
THE RAIN
POURED DOWN
and the
THUNDER CRASHED!

Jingles didn't know what to do...

The door opened waking Jingles a little.
Warm hands picked her up.
She felt a blanket around her and started
to feel warm and dry...

...She saw a **big black dog** staring at her.

THE
CHILDREN
PLAYED
and the fire
GLOWED,
THE EMBERS
CRACKED
and the
LIGHTS
TURNED LOW.

As she lay in the blanket she watched the warm glow
from the fire and enjoyed the heat.
"Don't worry little one. You are safe now,"
said the big black dog.

Jingles closed her eyes safe and snug.

She hoped this would be her new home.

THE WIND

DIED DOWN

and the

LIGHTNING

stoPPed...

THE RAIN

SLOWED

and the

THUNDER

DROPPED.

Book 2 in the Jingles Series coming soon for Christmas!

JINGLES AND HER AMAZING ADVENTURES
is a series of stories about Jingles,
a cute and curious terrier puppy.

Printed in Great Britain
by Amazon